THE MEDUSA PROJECT

LOU WILHAM

Midnight Tide
PUBLISHING

ALSO BY LOU WILHAM

The Curse Collection
    The Curse of The Black Cat
    The Curse of Ash and Blood

The Sea Witch Trilogy
    Tales of the Sea Witch

The Clockwork Chronicles
    The Girl in the Clockwork Tower
    The Unicorn and the Clockwork Quest

Villainous Heroics
    Villainous

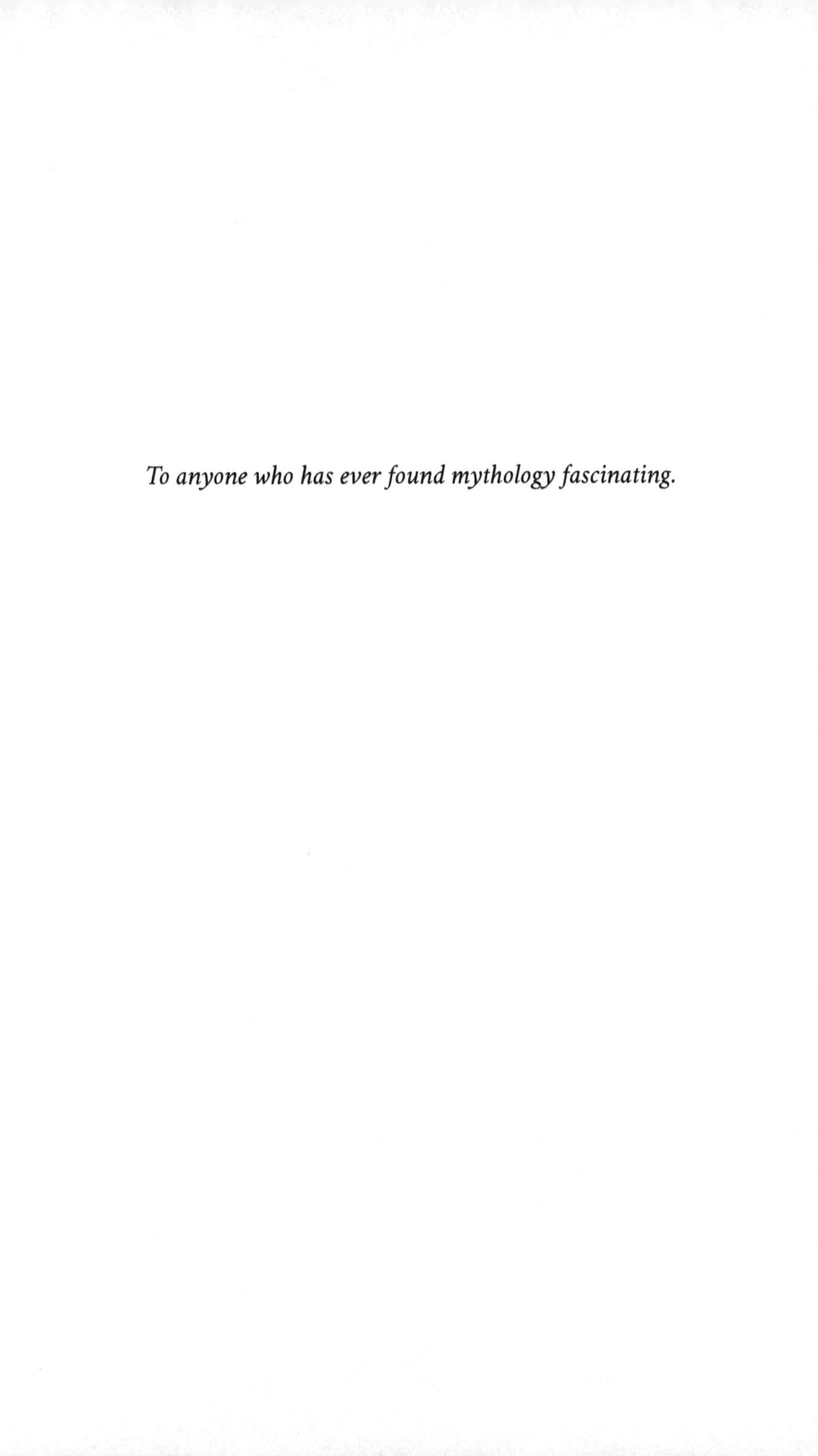

To anyone who has ever found mythology fascinating.

THE Medua Project

Lou Wilham

CHAPTER 1

EVERYONE TAKES things that don't belong to them. A dollar on the street. A pen at the bank. Another person's order at the coffee shop.

From Medusa, they took her reputation. From Poseidon, they took his freedom. And from this man …

"Agent Alcides," someone said, drawing Kyrie's attention back to the body. The man's neck was bent at an odd angle, made more evident by the stone beneath him holding his head up like a pillow.

From this man, they took his life.

"Yes, I'm listening," Kyrie said, drawing herself out of her own inner monologue long enough to crouch down beside the body. She pulled a pen from the messy bun perched on the back of her head and balanced a scrubby legal pad on her knee to take notes. "What do we know?"

"Henry Cadmus. Sixty-five. Retired Perseus agent."

Facts. It was easier for most humans to stick to the facts, to the black and white of a sheet of paper that listed who a person was in cold hard truths. Far easier to do that than to live in the strange world of color that Kyrie inhabited. But that's why she was good at her job.

"He's one of ours?" she asked. Pink ink scribbled in a messy scrawl across yellow paper, standing out in a way that looked more like two highlighters clashing than notes on a murder. She'd been told once not to use colored inks—it was unprofessional. Kyrie had ignored that suggestion and kept right on doing as she pleased. So long as she got results, she didn't see where it mattered what color she wrote in.

"Yeah. He retired pretty early. No one at the main office has seen him in at least twenty years."

Kyrie nodded, squinting up into the sun at the building looming above them. A modern thing, mostly windows that reflected the light in a hard glare, but the words up near the roof, emblazoned in crisp white sans-serif letters, were clear: Stone & Son's Excavation.

"Did he work here?" It was a silly question, or at least, most people would assume it was. Most people would assume that if a person somehow got access to the roof of a building, they must work there. Likewise, most people might assume this was a suicide. Kyrie was not most people.

"I'll have someone check the records."

"Can we move him yet?" She drew a neat little box around the words "Stone & Son's Excavation" on the pad. It meant something. A deliberate choice either by Cadmus himself or whoever had killed him.

"Not yet. The coroner wants to have a look-see."

"To make sure it's suicide?" Her pen made that weird springy sound as she tapped it against the pad.

"To make sure he wasn't killed first and then thrown off."

"Hmm," Kyrie hummed, standing from her crouch and taking turn about the body. It was strange where it had landed, and how. In a parking lot full of cars, Cadmus had missed them all and somehow landed on a rock the size of a pillow. There was no blood on the rock—that was even stranger. And his head was settled against it like he was sleeping, in spite of how the rest of his body was splayed in a mangled mess of broken bones. "He was moved."

"That's for the coroner to find out."

"No, that wasn't a question. He was definitely moved. This position was deliberate. Can we get him out of the way? I need a look at the rock." She tucked her pen back into the messy bun, ignoring the not-so-subtle yank of hard plastic in long hair.

"I told you, we have to wait for the coroner."

"Fine. How much longer will she be?"

"Twenty minutes."

Kyrie sighed, rocking back on her heels. Her hands fidgeted with the pad for a minute, feet tapping, before she got bored and wandered back toward her car.

"Where are you going?"

"I'm going to pull up Cadmus's Perseus records. Come get me when the coroner is done." She didn't even bother to turn back, just shouted loud enough for the whole parking lot to hear her. It took her a long minute of brushing away half-eaten french fries, fast food wrappers, and not-quite-empty cups of coffee in the back seat before she found her work bag buried under the mess. Crumpled files, half-used legal pads, and enough colorful pens to make an elementary school teacher blush fell into the passenger seat as she dug for her tablet. All the way to the bottom of the bag.

Tapping impatiently on the screen, she huffed when the big battery icon popped up, flashing red and angry.

"Okay. Okay. No need to shout." Thankfully, the charger was where it always was: plugged into the cigarette lighter along with a tangle of other cords. The car groaned at her as she turned the key before humming to life. More tapping followed as she waited for the tablet to charge up enough to be useful, along with the quiet chant of, "Charge. Charge. Charge."

A few other Perseus agents milled about, coming and going from the scene. None of them the coroner, which was a nuisance. How long did it take one person to arrive at a crime scene? And shouldn't the coroner have been there *first*?

After what seemed like forever, the screen came to life. Kyrie typed in her password, a twenty-digit monstrosity that the Perseus Initiative had chosen for her, and then quickly found her way into their app. More tapping, more impatient murmuring, as the little wheel spun and spun and spun.

"Hullo, Henry," she whispered, pushing her glasses up farther on her nose as her eyes skimmed the file. "Hmm. You were a busy boy, weren't you? Echo ... Antigone ... Achilles ... Medusa."

Kyrie's head cocked, a thought niggling at the back of her mind. Medusa, one of their first. The original victim Perseus had saved all those centuries ago. The great gorgon herself. A woman who could turn a man to stone with just a single sideways glance.

"Stone & Son's Excavation" glared back at Kyrie in bold pink letter.

"Well ... shit," Kyrie whispered. She turned off the car, dropped her tablet into the passenger seat, and headed back to the body.

"The coroner isn't—"

"When was Poseidon let out?" If Poseidon had been released, he was looking for Medusa. They had to get to her first.

The agent looked up from where he'd been tapping away at his own tablet and frowned. He turned back, fingers skidding against the glass until he had an answer. "A few weeks ago."

"Who is Medusa's handler? We need to warn them." She was already pulling her phone from her back pocket and tapping the green phone icon. "And I need Medusa's last known location."

"Medusa refused another handler after the last one." His scowl deepened, fingers clutching at the tablet. "We don't know where she is."

"Well, find her! Send me the address the moment you have it. And I need her number, whatever the last known contact was. If we don't have it, send me her sisters' numbers. We need to get in touch with her any way we can." Kyrie didn't stand around to wait. Her stride took her back to her car in quick, jarring steps.

"Where are you going?"

"To see Athena!"

CHAPTER 2

Coffee. Medusa needed coffee so she could function as a proper human being. Or proper gorgon being, rather. Not that it mattered one way or the other, they were so close to the same these days. So, she sipped, and she glared at the table, and she waited for the caffeine to kick in before her afternoon shift.

"Medusa?" a soft, feminine voice asked.

Medusa's glare rose from the strangely thick varnish of the table to the woman who dared address her before her afternoon coffee was finished. The woman in question was a mess, with a dark rat's nest of a bun haphazardly thrown atop her head and coming loose, a rumpled dress shirt that looked like she'd slept in it, and a pair of cat-eyed glasses, smudged, likely from being repeatedly pushed farther onto her face after sliding down her angular brow.

"I'm Kyrie," the woman said, holding out a hand sporting a bright blue ink stain on the thumb. "I'll be taking care of you."

"You?" The question held enough judgement that it would have made a lesser being cower. Kyrie, it seemed, was not a lesser being.

"Yes. Agent Kyrie Alcide." She held her hand in the air, stubbornly waiting for a handshake that would never come.

"Fantastic." Medusa lifted her coffee to take a long sip from the now lukewarm beverage. "Fan-tast-ic."

"Can we talk?" Kyrie pulled her hand back, finally, tucking it behind her back. She didn't look as miffed as she likely ought to, but Medusa decided she didn't care.

"We are talking."

Kyrie nodded and took the seat across from Medusa. Without an invitation. Bold choice.

"Poseidon is out," Kyrie said without preamble. She wasn't looking at Medusa, but instead digging through the bookbag covered in cute ice creams with faces all over it.

"And that affects me ... how?" Medusa tilted her head back to drain the coffee cup, reaching for her apron. "Can we hurry this up? My shift starts at five."

Kyrie looked up, confusion pinching her brows together. Medusa let out a long exhale and rolled her eyes.

"Okay. Fine. It's been a long time since I've done the whole song and dance. But you're cute, so I'll do it for you." Medusa sat up from her slouch, squaring her shoulders.

"What are you—"

"These children come here searching for glory and fame. All of them end the same. Tell me child, who sent you?" It was an old speech. Old and tired. Medusa hated it. But it was a part of the lore, as much as the 'snakes' for hair, and people liked the lore no matter how ridiculous it was. Maybe once it was done, the girl would bugger off. She pushed her own glasses up, the frames feeling unnaturally heavy with the weight they carried. The weight of protecting those around her from the stare of the gorgon.

Kyrie blinked at her for a moment, then snorted, then chortled. It was a gross laugh, and Medusa would have loved to lower her lenses if just to stop it. But she wouldn't.

She'd made a promise all those centuries ago, and she'd keep it.

"I'm sorry. I don't mean to laugh," Kyrie said, pulling her glasses from her face so she could brush at her wet eyes.

"Kind of sounds like you do," Medusa muttered, sullen.

"Is there more to it than that?" Kyrie's voice shook like she was holding back more snickers.

"Like I'd tell you."

"No … please?" Medusa wasn't sure how she'd done it, but Kyrie's eyes seemed to grow ten times bigger and take on the strange sheen of kittens, and puppies, and bunnies, and all things fluffy.

Medusa huffed and continued the speech she'd given every hero who ever thought themselves brave enough to face the gorgon. "That's what you want, isn't it? A monster to slay." The words felt silly then, but she'd say them, and get them out of the way so she didn't have to again. "Well, I hate to break it to you sweetie, but in this world, we're all monsters."

Kyrie's composure broke again, her hands flying to her mouth to muffle the sound. They couldn't. It took a long time for her to regain control, but when she did, she shook her head.

"Like I was saying before you got all …" Kyrie waved her hand to gesture to the general all of Medusa that there was. Medusa bit down on a biting retort, teeth sinking into her tongue to hold it. "Poseidon is out. Henry Cadmus is dead. He was thrown off the top of Stone & Son's Excavation, and then laid out on a couple of rocks like some kind of …" She faltered, then shrugged. "Doesn't matter. Point is, you were Cadmus's last job."

"Cadmus?" Medusa's fingers tightened around her empty cup, denting it a little at the palm.

"So we need to get you back into hiding. I've got a room

all booked for us already." Kyrie hadn't stopped talking. She didn't seem to notice that Medusa was having trouble swallowing around a lump. "We leave now."

"My shift …"

"I've spoken to your employer. We'll drop by my place to pick up my go-bag, and then you can get whatever you need brought to you by one of your sisters."

Medusa nodded numbly. She lost track of everything after that. The walk to the car, the drive to the apartment, the ride in the elevator. It all turned into a strange blur that slipped through her fingers every time she tried to hold it, like light, or water, or sand. It wasn't until she was standing at the window in Kyrie's mess of an apartment that she finally came to.

She blinked down at a row of succulents along the windowsill. Some had clearly browned with rot, and others were in varying stages of shriveling up from dehydration. *And this*, she thought a little sourly, *is who they assigned to protect me?*

"Oh, don't mind those." Kyrie laughed as she stuffed what looked like a box of paints into a bag. "I thought if I could keep them alive for a while then I could maybe graduate to a cat."

"How's that working for you?"

With a glance at the plants, Kyrie's face twisted into something bordering on sardonic. "Not well."

What followed was another blur of motion. Distantly, Medusa was aware that they had checked into a motel on the outskirts of town. But she wasn't sure when, or what time it was. All she was sure of was that she was there now. Sitting at the table, looking out the window at a parking lot as she waited for Kyrie to come back with a burner phone from the Perseus Initiative so she could call her sisters.

She needed someone to feed the cat, she told herself.

Everything else could be left behind or replaced. Which …
she wondered what that said about the life she'd built for
herself in Lore. Flitting from one of Athena's coffee shops to
another, to a bar, and back. She supposed she could build the
exact same life anywhere else.

It wouldn't make a difference.

CHAPTER 3

"You're in all the textbooks, you know," Kyrie said, folding her piece of pizza in half and taking a bite. The crust tasted like cardboard, but she wasn't willing to take the risk of having the pizza place across town deliver to the motel. "They teach us about your case first."

"As a prime example of victim blaming, I assume," Medusa muttered, peeling a pepperoni off her own slice. Kyrie hadn't thought to ask if Medusa liked pepperoni, and now it was too little too late.

"No. Well … that too." Kyrie shifted uncomfortably in the T-shirt she'd pulled from her go-bag. It was worn and wrinkled in all the wrong places, with the Perseus logo on the right breast. "But it's mostly because you were the first. You came out, and then there was this flood of people testifying against the gods. We were able to put away Zeus and Hera. And even Hermes for a couple of decades."

The cheese made a wet squelching sound as Medusa peeled off another piece of greasy meat and set it onto Kyrie's plate without a word. Kyrie made a mental note to try something else next time. Maybe pineapple and ham? She wasn't sure, but she'd rather get something Medusa liked.

"So what?" Medusa asked when it seemed like the silence would stretch on forever.

"You're a hero." It sounded ridiculous, and earnest, and bordering on fangirl manic even to Kyrie's own ears, but there it was. The moment she'd seen Medusa's name on Cadmus's file, she'd rushed to her. It wasn't just about protecting Medusa, it was to meet her. To have a chance at getting to know one of the bravest—

"I'm not a hero." Medusa's tone was bored, her gaze fixed on the laminate table between them. The clear lenses of her glasses reflected the yellow overhead light, making it hard to read those forest-green eyes. Jade hair, forest eyes. *Pretty,* Kyrie had thought the first time they'd looked into her own. Pretty, and deadly.

"It was brave. You're brave."

"For what? Getting a god locked up for a couple centuries?" She dropped her slice back onto the plate in front of her with a slap. "What's a couple centuries to a god?"

Kyrie took another big bite to buy herself time. The cheese stuck to the roof of her mouth. Medusa waited, watching her, one brow lifted on her brown face. Kyrie swallowed the half-chewed hunk of crust; it scraped on the way down.

"A couple centuries can do a lot of damage," she argued once she was sure it wouldn't come out as a croak.

Medusa tilted her head. A jade loc fell from beneath the hood of the sweatshirt she'd stolen from Kyrie's bag. It fit her a little more snuggly than it had Kyrie, but who was paying attention to that? No one.

"You don't believe me."

"No. I don't. You're a human. What would you know about the damage time can do to gods?"

"Humans have short memories." Kyrie grabbed another

slice from the box between them and folded it just as she had the first. "And without constant reinforcement, things that they once believed in become myth. You don't see humans praying to Zeus anymore. Or bowing before Hera."

"You don't see them doing that to Athena either, and she seems to be doing all right."

"Athena adapted. She built a business for herself instead of relying on prayers." Kyrie shrugged. "I'm not saying they can't bounce back, but it'll be harder for a god who has been out of the world for so long. That's all."

"They teach you shit like that in Perseus?" Medusa shoved her plate away, curling her knees up onto the chair. "Seems stupidly optimistic."

"We have to believe that what we're doing makes a difference, or we wouldn't do it."

Medusa laughed, a low, dark sound, rich with centuries of pain, and loss, and missing out, but no less beautiful for it. It made Kyrie's insides ache, like she should reach over and hug Medusa. Like she could hold the other woman together by sheer force of will. But she didn't think that would be well received, so she stayed where she was.

"What?" she asked instead.

"Recognizing that …" Medusa breathed, reaching for her bottled water. "Doesn't it make it harder?"

"You'd think. But not really."

They sat in silence for a while after that. Kyrie polished off a third slice, and Medusa stared at the table. It was uncomfortable in the way that two people sitting in a dingy motel was uncomfortable. And that awkwardness slowly ate away at Kyrie's resolve to not make the whole thing weirder than it already was.

"You did all right for yourself," her mouth said, bypassing the filter between it and her brain entirely. Kyrie kept her eyes on the table between them, thankful that without her glasses, everything was slightly out of focus. She felt Medusa's eyes narrow on her but refused to let the other woman make her squirm. She'd started, now she may as well finish. "You're like … a feminist icon."

"What?"

"They put you on T-shirts and write poems about you and stuff."

"Who does?"

"Humans. Women." Kyrie squeezed her eyes shut, willing her mouth to stop running, but it wasn't going to. She knew better than that. She'd never been able to stop it before; why should now be any different? "Specifically, women who've been …" She swallowed the word, not wanting to say it out loud.

Medusa growled.

"It's a good thing," Kyrie argued, lifting her head to look at Medusa. She was met with a cold hard stare. "It gives people hope."

"So that's it then." Medusa scoffed, looking away from her.

"What's it?"

"I get to be some … some … *symbol*." Medusa spat the word like a slur. "What happened to me is okay, acceptable, because it let other people prosper? I should be happy because at least it meant I got to help others when they needed it? Because it turned me into some kind of feminist figurehead?"

Kyrie flinched at the words. Her hands gripped hard onto the edge of the table. "I didn't … I didn't say that!"

"What *did* you say?" Medusa's feet hit the floor, her body perching on the edge of the metal chair.

"I … I don't know …"

Medusa snorted, standing, and headed for the door.

"Where are you going?"

"To get some air!" Then she slammed the door behind her, and Kyrie heard hard footsteps down the length of the hall.

"Good job, Kyrie," she muttered to herself. She flung back in the chair to stare up at the ceiling tiles. "Good job."

CHAPTER 4

THE ROOM WAS dark but for the light in the bathroom when Medusa returned. Kyrie Alcides was in a lump, curled up into the fetal position on the bed closest to the door. Medusa had the thought to wake her but decided against it. It had been a long day, and all she wanted was to pour herself into bed and just not think for a little while. So she did, letting the inky darkness of the blackout curtains lull her to sleep.

What felt like minutes later, a loud buzzing woke Medusa. It took her brain a moment to parse together where she was and what she was hearing. When she looked up, Kyrie's phone was skittering across the nightstand between them.

"Alcides … Alcides …" Medusa huffed, grabbing a pillow from behind her and throwing it at the other woman. "Kyrie!"

"Huh? What?" Kyrie blinked awake, her eyes still heavily lidded.

"Your phone!" Medusa hissed. She grabbed the still vibrating device from the table and chucked it at Kyrie. The intent had been to smack Kyrie in the face with it, but Kyrie caught the damn thing easily.

"Alcides," Kyrie said once she'd held it up to her ear. Her face twisted into … something. Confusion maybe. She blinked hard, her nose scrunching up. Then there was a sudden shift, something Medusa hadn't seen very often on humans whose emotions took a longer time to switch, but oh so often on immortals who had spent centuries turning themselves to steel. Kyrie's expression sharpened, her blue eyes hardening as she sat up straighter. "Yes. She's with me, sir."

The muffled voice on the other end said something else, and Kyrie nodded.

"Send me the address. I'll be there in ten." Then she hung up and stood to get dressed.

"What was that all about?" Medusa flopped back against her pillows.

"Get dressed." Kyrie pulled a hair tie from her wrist and started wrangling her brown hair up into another untidy bun.

"Why?"

"We have a crime scene to get to." She looked right at Medusa when she said those words, as if gauging Medusa's reaction. Maybe she was.

"I repeat: Why?" Medusa raised her brows, only a little put out by the commanding tone coming from Kyrie.

"Because I have to go, and I can't leave you here alone. Put some pants on. Let's go."

Kyrie didn't say anything else; she just gathered her things. Medusa got dressed before following obediently to the messy car.

"Who died?" Medusa asked once they were on the road. She'd leaned forward to try and reset Kyrie's clock, which was an hour and twenty minutes off somehow.

Kyrie, to her credit, didn't flinch at the blunt question.

She did glance over a Medusa, measuring her response again. "Poseidon."

"Oh." Medusa's shoulders fell, her face going carefully blank when she couldn't immediately identify the emotion rolling inside of her. Was she sad? No, not really. Was she surprised? Yes. Was she relieved? Also, undoubtedly, yes. But there was something else too. Worry, maybe? Guilt? Shame? Yes … perhaps it was shame at the relief. No one should be relieved that another person was dead. "But he's a—"

"A god, yes." Kyrie nodded. "It wasn't an easy thing to do. It looks like someone drowned him in cement and left him there. And with so little belief in him left from being in prison …"

That was … Medusa let out a long, slow breath as she stared out through the windshield. That was one hell of a way to go.

"I'm free to go then, right? He's the one who killed Cadmus. If he's gone, then I'm safe." Finally, her emotions settled on something closer to, if not happiness, at least satisfaction. She could go home to her cat, and her life. She didn't have to live at the dingy motel with Kyrie. Still, it wasn't just that. It wasn't just the motel. It was the hiding. She'd been hiding for centuries. She'd been running from her past for forever, even before she'd testified against Poseidon. And now … Now she was finally going to get some peace.

"Medusa, I need to ask you something, and I need you to be honest with me."

Medusa's brows knit at the serious note in Kyrie's voice, but she turned to look at her with a nod.

"Where did you go last night?" Kyrie was gripping the steering wheel hard, her knuckles turning white with the pressure.

"What?" Medusa blinked, shook her head, and blinked again. "What do you mean …" And then it all came to her in a rush. "Oh. They think I did this. And then what? Called it in?"

Of course they did. Poseidon had … He'd hurt her, and a few centuries in prison wasn't enough to make up for that. They all knew what a gorgon's vengeance could be like. But if she'd wanted to kill him …

"Look, if I wanted that bastard dead, I wouldn't have used cement. I'd have turned him to stone and been done with it. That's much easier than wasting time and energy figuring out how to tie up a god and hold him down long enough to drown him." Medusa snorted, crossing her arms over her chest.

"You didn't want him dead?"

"No. I did. I definitely did." Medusa sighed. She turned to look out the window on the passenger side. Lore was passing them through the glass. The city was sharp, and white, and modern against the early morning sun. Its glare burned her eyes. "I'm just saying, I wouldn't have done it that way."

"That makes sense," Kyrie said, like it genuinely did. Her turn signal clicked to life, and she pulled off into a parking lot.

"It does?"

Kyrie nodded.

"Where are we?" Medusa looked up at the black building. It didn't have a name painted on the outside, or any kind of signage. It was just a black building, stark amongst the sea of white. Nothing more. "I thought we were going to a crime scene."

"If I take you to the scene, they're going to arrest you." Kyrie's tone had gone soft, patient.

"Why?"

"Poseidon was killed before Cadmus. Weeks ago, in fact." Kyrie pulled out her phone to check something, then nodded. "They found some of your hair in the cement in his lungs."

"They *what?*"

Kyrie didn't answer. She waited for those facts to settle into Medusa's mind. When they did, Medusa scowled.

"Someone is framing me. You believe me … don't you?"

"I want to." Kyrie let out a long breath, her shoulders sagging with some invisible weight. How did humans manage to carry so much of the world on their shoulders and not fold under the pressure of it? Not the knowledge, no. The responsibility. As if every human was responsible for the state of the world around them. Medusa would never understand.

"But?"

"But the evidence doesn't look good."

"You're going to let them arrest me." It wasn't a question; it was a foregone conclusion. Something Medusa would have to come to terms with … eventually.

"I didn't say that." Kyrie dropped her phone into her lap and met Medusa's gaze again.

"What are you saying?"

"I'm saying this bar is owned by an old family friend. Go in. Have a drink. I'll come pick you up around lunch."

"And if I run?"

Kyrie laughed, sharp and short, and then said dead seriously, "I'll find you. But if you're innocent, you don't have any reason to run."

Medusa nodded and climbed out of the car on legs that felt oddly like jelly. She looked back at Kyrie through the windshield. Kyrie nodded toward the door, and Medusa made her way inside the dark bar.

CHAPTER 5

Trusting Medusa was instinct. An instinct Kyrie decided to not look too closely at. It was better that way. The moment a person tried to understand that internal thing that told them a thing was right or wrong was the moment logic ripped it apart. Because what she'd done, she realized as she drove away from the bar, was not logical.

All signs pointed to Medusa as the prime suspect. She had motive, means, and opportunity. Add to that the hair which had been found inside the body, and it was a solid case. But something didn't feel right about it to Kyrie. They hadn't found any of Medusa's hair on Cadmus. And Medusa had been upset to learn of the man's passing. Sure, she could have been faking that, but grief, actual grief, was hard to fake.

The pieces just didn't fit.

And Kyrie hadn't been lying when she'd told Medusa that if she ran, Kyrie would catch her. That was the nature of a Perseus agent's job, to catch the mythical, and Kyrie was damn good at her job.

Still, she saw the look of unease that passed over the other agents when she arrived at the garbage heap where Poseidon had been disposed of. The body had been taken away, but everything else was still in place. The barrel which had been cut open to remove him lay in pieces on the ground amongst the refuse.

"Who called it in?" Kyrie asked, crouching next to a particularly large chunk of cement.

"It was an anonymous tip." The agent's voice was heavy, like he was trying not to breathe through his nose. "Where is the suspect?"

"You let me worry about Medusa." Kyrie pulled a pen from her hair to scribble some notes across a bent legal pad. She sketched the bit of white logo on the barrel that she could see, then moved to take in more of it, fitting the pieces together like a puzzle in her head. "Stone & Son's. Again."

"A clear message from Medusa," another agent said. She had red hair. *Carmine, actually*, Kyrie thought. She'd been with Perseus for a long time; Kyrie could always tell. It was the way her chin tipped back in superiority. They got this air about themselves at some point, like they knew better than the rest of the world just because they hunted monsters for a living.

"It's not Medusa." Kyrie rose to her feet, kicking a bit of cement aside to take in the clear indent left from the barrel. The trash had built up around it over time, although how much she couldn't tell, as it'd all been moved to clear a path to the scene. "Do we have any pictures from the scene before you removed the barrel?"

"They're in the file," came the huffed response from the young man again. He looked quite ill, a green tone settling into his cheeks. He'd probably already thrown up once, if the way he swayed was anything to go by.

Kyrie nodded.

"What do you mean it's not Medusa?" the red-haired agent asked. *Carmine*, Kyrie's mind supplied again, even if it wasn't her name. "We found her hair in his lungs, Alcides. His lungs! It has to be her."

"It doesn't have to be anyone." Kyrie shrugged, pulling out her phone to browse the pictures in the file.

"What's that supposed to mean?"

"It means that if it were Medusa, and she didn't want to get caught, she wouldn't have called in a tip."

"How do you know it was the killer who called in the tip?" the young man piped up, his face going from nauseous to earnest.

"Do you regularly go digging through garbage heaps looking for murder victims in cemented-shut barrels?"

"Well … no."

"This is about your crush," Carmine accused, her finger pointed threateningly at Kyrie. "You've always had a thing for that one. And now you're deliberately—"

"I'm not deliberately doing anything other than my job," Kyrie cut her off, eyes narrowed. "None of this makes sense, and Medusa is innocent until proven otherwise."

"The hairs—"

"The hairs! The hairs!" Kyrie laughed high and falsetto, bordering on manic, and shook her head quick enough to dislodge a pen from the bun. "The hairs could be pulled off her hairbrush, or taken from her clothes, or ripped from her head at work. She works in customer service. She comes in contact with hundreds of people every day. Any one of those people could have gotten some of her hair and shoved it into some cement."

"Who would go through that kind of hassle?" Carmine snorted, rolling her eyes. "You aren't going to bring her in for questioning then?"

"I am, in fact. I just wasn't going to bring her to a crime scene where she could contaminate evidence." Kyrie had never been a particularly good liar, but this was at least partly true. She didn't want Medusa contaminating the scene. She *was* going to question Medusa. It was just that questioning wasn't likely to happen in an interrogation room. Kyrie would decide what to do with Medusa after her questions had been answered.

"Then you won't mind telling us where she is."

"She's with a friend."

Carmine nodded skeptically. "I want her back at headquarters before this evening."

"Yeah. We'll see you then." Kyrie turned to pick her way back to her car. Once there, she allowed herself a singular moment of panic. She had lied to another Perseus agent. It didn't matter that Carmine wasn't her superior. It didn't matter that it wasn't entirely a lie. If she were caught, she'd be in a world of trouble.

Once that thought had filtered through her mind, she forced it aside, gripped the steering wheel, and headed back to the bar.

By the time she'd reached the black building, she'd made up her mind.

CHAPTER 6

It was too early to drink.

But those rules didn't apply to women who had learned the man who'd raped them and ruined their lives was dead. Nor did they apply to women who'd been accused of murder. Those rules applied to normal women. Women who got up in the morning, got dressed, and went to work. Women who had boyfriends or girlfriends. Women who didn't spend their lives trying to pretend like they didn't exist at all.

So, instead of ordering what could pass for coffee at the hole-in-the-wall bar from the bartender with the beautiful, winged eyeliner, she ordered a gin and coke. At least she was getting some caffeine in her system, right?

When that one was gone, she ordered another. And then another.

By the time the door opened, flooding the dimly lit, empty bar with mid-morning sunlight, she was well and truly buzzed, and the bartender had given up trying to uncomfortably edge toward the back room. It wasn't the ideal way to deal with what was going on in her life, and she wouldn't have recommended it to anyone, but she didn't know how else to handle this turn of events.

"And then," Medusa said, leaning forward to smirk at the bartender who was giving her a worried look. "They told everyone I had snakes for hair!" She threw her head back and cackled, long and loud and unhinged.

"I think you should switch to water."

"Not snakes," she continued as if he hadn't spoken. She grabbed one of the green locs draped over her shoulder. "No. Not snakes. Braids. Well … sort of."

"But they were always green, weren't they?" he asked, and he seemed genuinely curious. He wasn't looking at her anymore, and she didn't have to wonder why when Kyrie came to take the stool beside her.

"Yeah, I guess." She shrugged. "Water?"

"Water." He nodded, then grabbed a glass and filled it from the tap behind the bar. It thunked lightly against the wood in front of her. "Kyrie."

"Elijah," said Kyrie. "Don't go too far. I've got work for you."

Elijah nodded, shooting Kyrie a mischievous smile before disappearing into the back room.

"You didn't run." Kyrie stepped onto the rungs of her barstool so she could lean over the bar to grab a glass, fill it with clear soda, and drop a handful of cherries into it.

"I'm innocent," Medusa replied flatly, taking a deep gulp of water. Already the softness of alcohol was beginning to fade. Such was the curse of an immortal. Without it, the events of the last few hours came back into sharp focus. Poseidon was dead, but she was not out of danger.

"You are," Kyrie agreed. She plucked the stem off a cherry and popped it into her mouth to chew thoughtfully.

"You believe me?"

"You've given me no reason not to." Kyrie's tone was simple, like she was stating facts or reading from a menu instead of telling Medusa that she wasn't a murderer. It was the same tone her predecessor had used all those centuries ago, when the hero Perseus said he believed her that what Poseidon had done wasn't her fault. And it dredged up the same age-old feeling that Medusa still didn't have a name for. She was embarrassed to admit her eyes were burning with tears.

"What now?"

Kyrie didn't answer in words. Instead, she pulled her dismantled Perseus cell phone from a pocket on her bag and set the pieces carefully on the bar. The screen wasn't cracked, but she'd pulled the battery and all the important bits out of it. It was now a useless pile of metal and glass.

Medusa blinked down at the innards of the phone, trying to understand what she was seeing. She'd never actually known someone to pull their own smartphone apart. It was something done in the back room of a smartphone store, not in the car on the way to a bar. Kyrie slid a little circuit board toward Medusa as if it meant something.

"What am I looking at?" she asked when she couldn't really make sense of it.

"The GPS chip," Elijah supplied helpfully. He'd returned from the back room with a laptop under his arm and two flip phones in hard plastic shells in his hands.

"Why is it outside of the phone?"

Elijah blinked at her like she was stupid. Maybe she was. It was starting to feel like she was. Then he set the laptop on the bar top and grabbed a pair of scissors to open the pre-paid phones. "I've got you a backdoor already."

"Elijah, you charmer." Kyrie laughed, leaning forward to grab the laptop from him, and began to type away at some-thing. "How did you know?"

"I can read between the lines." He snorted, setting both phones on the bar and plugging them in behind it to charge.

"These are your new phones. They are only for contacting people you trust."

"Just you," Kyrie mumbled distractedly around a cherry stem.

"Exactly."

Medusa looked between them, her brows creasing, a headache forming between them. "What's going on?"

"We're taking your case." Elijah reached over to refill Kyrie's cup.

"My case? What case?"

Kyrie huffed, straightening up from over the laptop to look at Medusa blandly. "The case of who killed Poseidon, and Cadmus, and is trying to frame you for it."

"Oh … Okay."

Kyrie nodded and returned to her hunch, her shoulders rounding as her finger moved across the track pad. "I'm not seeing anything new here. I know all of this."

"Check the back files," Elijah said. He'd opened both flip phones and was busy typing away at them. Medusa wasn't sure what he was doing. Maybe adding contacts?

"The back files," Kyrie muttered. A couple more clicks on the keyboard and then she sat up, suddenly more alert. "Huh. Now that's interesting."

"Thought you'd like that." Elijah chuckled.

"Did you get me everything I need?"

Elijah scoffed, rolling his eyes. "What do you take me for? Some kind of amateur?"

He went back to the back room and came out again with two bags full of different sized, shaped, and colored noodles.

"Ah! I love you!" Kyrie crowed. She grabbed the bags from him, laptop forgotten as plastic crinkled under seeking fingers, inspecting her haul. "You're the best."

"You know, I haven't seen you this excited about a case since you were a rookie." He made it sound conversational, but there was a keen look in his eyes that said it was more than that. Kyrie didn't seem to notice.

"What do you need noodles for?" Medusa felt like she was only getting half of this conversation, and she didn't like it. The not knowing was stressful, and she felt that stress settle achingly at the base of her skull.

"For solving the case." Kyrie looked up from the bag with a gleam in her eyes. "Elijah was in training with me as a rookie."

"Before I dropped out," he added.

"And we figured out that crafty stuff helps me think."

"So … noodles?" Medusa prompted, still feeling strangely bereft and more concerned now than ever about laying her fate in the hands of someone who needed noodles to solve a murder.

"Macaroni art!" Elijah cheered.

Kyrie went back to inspecting her "art supplies," lining the boxes up on the bar so she could take in the different shapes.

"I'm dead. Aren't I?" Medusa asked, not expecting an answer.

"Nah, you'll be all right." Elijah winked at her. "Kyrie's weird, but she gets results."

CHAPTER 7

With the gift cards Elijah had gotten them—paid for with cash, of course—Kyrie was able to reserve them another dingy little motel room.

"You can take the first shower," she told Medusa as she moved to kneel on the worn carpet in front of the queen bed. She opened each box of noodles, setting them side by side so she could see what kind they were on the side of the box. With the sound of the shower in the background, Kyrie started to glue them together, making little mandalas from bowtie pasta to get started, and a face from elbow noodles.

She was so wrapped up in her work that she didn't notice when the shower turned off and Medusa rejoined her.

"There's one thing I still don't get." Medusa's voice broke through the relative hush of the highway just outside.

"Just one thing?" Kyrie asked, not looking up from her work creating a small replica of the barrel from tortellini. She was used to her methods being questioned. In fact, she hadn't been able to create a proper noodle landscape since she'd been a rookie because she hated the weird looks she got in the office. It was better to just sketch things in different colored inks and pretend not to notice how much easier it would be if she were allowed to create sculptures instead. "It's not the noodles, is it?"

"No. It's not." Medusa shook her head and paused before adding, "I don't really get that either."

Kyrie shrugged. "Sculpture helps me think, and macaroni art is cleaner than clay."

"Okay. I get that." Medusa nodded. She sat down beside Kyrie, her legs folded like a pretzel and her hands in her lap, looking at the few pieces Kyrie had created so far.

"What is it you don't get?" Kyrie asked, finishing up the little barrel and setting it amongst a pile of random other noodles. She grabbed a box of linguine to start putting together a miniature Stone & Son's Excavation building.

Medusa was quiet for a long time, handing Kyrie noodles when she asked for them and just watching the process of building a skyscraper from dry pasta. When Kyrie perched the little noodle building next to the gnocchi and rigatoni body of Henry Cadmus, she looked back to Medusa. Medusa's dark lips were pressed together into a tight line, brows creased at the center behind her glasses.

"What is it you don't get?" Kyrie asked again, her voice soft.

Medusa let out a breath, her shoulders slumping forward. She didn't meet Kyrie's eyes, but Kyrie didn't expect her to. Not really.

"I don't get why you're helping me." Medusa's voice was quiet, almost like if she said the words loud enough, Kyrie would realize what a stupid idea all of this was. She wouldn't. Kyrie may have been the type to jump in headfirst, but she never once regretted a decision once she'd made it.

"I'm going to order ramen for dinner. Elijah said there's a really good place around the corner. What kind do you want?" Kyrie said. She knew it wasn't an answer, not to the question Medusa was asking, anyway. But she didn't have a good answer. So instead of trying to think of one, she stretched her arms over her head, elbows popping from too long gluing noodles together, and went to grab her phone.

"What—Whatever they have that's vegetarian." Medusa stumbled over the words, her eyes round as she watched Kyrie dial a number off a pamphlet that Elijah had tucked in amongst the noodle boxes.

Kyrie nodded. "Call your sisters and have them pick up anything you need from your apartment. I'm sure this place doesn't have your normal hair products."

"Okay." Medusa sounded like she maybe wanted to argue, but she went to grab the other burner phone. Kyrie ducked out as she was dialing.

ട്

She met the delivery boy around the corner, ignoring the confused look he gave her, and then headed back to their room. Medusa was waiting for her, looking down over the noodle reproduction of Henry Cadmus's murder.

"See anything?" Kyrie asked, dropping onto the queen bed. She opened the paper bag and pulled out two plastic containers along with chopsticks.

"No. I've never heard of Stone & Son's."

"I didn't think you had." Kyrie patted the bed beside her. "Come sit. We'll go over some of the back files Elijah gave us."

"We're going to eat on the bed?" Medusa eyed the garish motel coverlet with her nose curled.

"We don't have a table." Kyrie shrugged. She grabbed the laptop from the nightstand and opened it. Her finger jiggled across the trackpad until the screen came to life.

Medusa sat beside her, making the containers slosh a little. Kyrie passed her a set of chopsticks and the dug into her own food as she scrolled through the file of Jillian Barnabus.

"I know her," Medusa said around a mouthful of bock choy. "She was my handler … thirteen years ago? What happened to her?"

Kyrie frowned, swallowing a chunk of pork noisily. She debated for a moment what she should tell Medusa. The gorgon hadn't taken Cadmus's death well; Kyrie doubted she'd be pleased to know that more of her handlers had died. Ultimately, logic won out. Medusa needed to know so they could figure out who was framing her.

"They found her body last week at a quarry," Kyrie said softly. She put the container of noodles in between her thighs to keep it from spilling and reached to pat Medusa's knee awkwardly.

Medusa's expression went blank. She nodded, but her food sat forgotten in her lap. "So they … There are more of them."

"Yes." Kyrie tried to say it as gently as she could, but she couldn't lie. "Four total, including Cadmus and Barnabus."

"Who would do that?" Medusa sounded small. So small. Kyrie could understand the guilt that lined Medusa's eyes, dragging her lips down into sadness.

"I don't know. But we're going to find out."

Medusa reached to take the hand that Kyrie had left on her knee, squeezing her fingers almost painfully. Then she nodded again. "Okay."

"Good." Kyrie offered what she hoped was an encouraging smile. "We should get some sleep soon."

"Why?" Medusa grabbed the lid for her food, sealing it up. It wasn't even a quarter of the way empty, but Kyrie supposed she had a right to not be hungry after that.

"In the morning, we're going to go to all the scenes. I need to see them with my own eyes to make sense of them." She also thought Medusa could use the rest, but she didn't say as much. She didn't want Medusa to think she was coddling her. Even if she was.

CHAPTER 8

Medusa didn't know a lot about crime scenes—only that if she ever saw another one, it would be too soon—but she was pretty sure the ones they had seen that morning hadn't offered anything useful. Well, other than the killer's fondness for businesses involving stone of some kind. Which was clearly a message. Whether it was meant as threat or a taunt, Medusa felt reasonably sure it was both.

They weren't done until after lunchtime, and then Kyrie drove them to the black building again.

"Won't they be looking for you here?" Medusa asked.

"Maybe. But I doubt it. Elijah fell off the map after he left Perseus. Something about realizing how easy it was to track a person using their electronic footprint." Kyrie shrugged, killing the engine. "He's not wrong, of course. It's wicked easy, but that's no reason to be paranoid."

"Isn't it?"

"Pft … maybe." Kyrie chuckled softly, leaning back in her seat. "Come on. Let's go in. He makes a really good BLT."

The bar, which Medusa still hadn't learned the name of, was empty again. She wondered how Elijah could afford to keep it open all day when there were no customers in sight but decided not to ask. Some questions were best left as just that: questions. Its restrooms were well-lit, single-stall rooms. Medusa ran the water as hot as it would go—scalding—and grabbed the soap.

She hadn't seen any bodies, but she felt like she had blood on her hands. Four humans had died because of her. How many would it be in the end, by the time they found whoever was framing her? Five? A dozen? More? She scrubbed harder at her skin, ignoring the way the hot water made it prickle.

When she finally turned the water off, her hands were flushed pink with heat, and the skin around the knuckles was raw. But she still felt it there. That sticky, buzzing feeling of blood, even where there was none. She took a second to close her eyes and breathe, focusing instead on the soft hum of voices in the bar.

"Crime scenes are not first date material, Kyrie," Elijah said. It sounded like he was choking back laughter.

"What?" Kyrie asked.

There was silence. A conversation with just facial expressions. Probably the lifting of a well-plucked eyebrow, and a little smirk on Elijah's part. Followed by a gaping Kyrie.

"It's not … That wasn't … We are not dating!"

Well, that was enough of that. Medusa opened the bathroom door noisily to let them know she was coming back out. She looked over at Kyrie, who had gone an interesting shade of red.

"We didn't find anything this morning," Medusa said to fill the space that had been left from the pair being caught talking about her. "The scenes were clean."

"I've got plenty of pictures in the files." Kyrie deflated, her eyes flicking away to stare at the rows of liquor behind the bar. "It's not ideal, but it will do. Those photographers never get all the details."

Elijah snorted and rolled his eyes.

"What? They don't!" Kyrie huffed. The blush was fading from her cheeks, but it remained stubbornly at the tips of her ears. Medusa wondered how long they'd sit there pretending that the conversation hadn't happened.

"Lunch will be up soon." Elijah went back to drying a stack of damp glasses and stocking them behind the bar. "You want it to go?"

"No." Medusa shook her head. She knew it wasn't safe for them to be out in the open like they were, but she didn't think she could go back to being cooped up in that room. Not with Kyrie. Not yet. "Euryale sent Stheno over to my place to pick up some of my things. She'll be by tonight to drop them off."

"I get to meet Stheno?" That perked Kyrie up. Medusa wasn't sure how she felt about that. She decided to shelve it to think on later.

"Yeah. I guess you do."

Lunch was a quiet affair after that. Kyrie went back over everything she'd learned at the scenes, creating sketches in lime green on the bar napkins of the buildings surrounding the murders. Medusa enjoyed what little peace there was to be had.

A loud electronic screaming sound, like an alarm clock having a stroke, broke the silence just as they were finishing up.

"What the hell is that?" Medusa cringed, covering her ears with her hands.

Elijah pulled a phone from his pocket and hit the button the side to silence it. Then he smiled sheepishly at them.

"That's not a good noise," Kyrie said, bracing herself on the bar so she could lean over her empty plate to get a better look at the little screen. Her T-shirt trailed through what was left of the ketchup on her plate, but Medusa didn't bother to stop her.

Elijah paled as he scanned the alert.

"Elijah. What is it?"

"Did you leave your stuff at the motel?" he asked, voice carefully neutral.

"I grabbed my go-bag, but all my art is there." Kryie sat back in her seat, nose wrinkling. "Why?"

"I'll grab whatever is left." Elijah held out his hand for the keycard, and Kyrie passed it over. "You two stay here, lock the door behind me, and turn off the Open sign. I'll be back soon."

Kyrie was already up and moving before he'd finished speaking.

"Elijah …" Medusa felt her shoulders clench up around her ears, the food in her stomach turning heavy. "What is it?"

He shook his head and left, not answering her question. Kyrie locked the door behind him, then pulled the shade down so no one could see inside.

"There's been another murder," Kyrie said when every- thing was settled per Elijah's instructions. She turned to face Medusa, her expression harder than Medusa had ever seen it. "The body was found around the corner from the motel where we were staying. In the parking lot of a company that specializes in granite countertops."

"Who … Who was it?" Medusa felt the lead in her stomach sink, tugging it down toward her toes, then back up to writhe at the back of her throat. She was going to be sick. Oh gods, she was going to be sick.

"We don't know yet. Medusa … Medusa drink some water. Breathe. You're having a panic attack. Just breathe …"

Medusa could only just hear Kyrie's words over the pounding of her pulse in her ears. But she let the other woman take her hands and ground her. Let the warmth and callouses of those long, elegant fingers keep her from floating away like a balloon.

CHAPTER 9

Elijah was back within the hour, but he didn't open the bar back up upon arrival. Instead, he slid a key from his key ring across the polished wood surface.

"I need your phones. There are new ones in the car."

Kyrie nodded, pulling the flip phone from her pocket and popping the battery out without having to be told. "Have you got another card for us to use?"

"In the car." Elijah took the pieces of the phone, set them in the sink, plugged it, and turned on the water.

"What's going on?" Medusa's lips twitched, eyes flicking between them. She looked jittery, nervous, and Kyrie wished there was something she could do to help, but she knew there wasn't. The best solution was to put some distance between themselves and that scene.

"We're moving motels," Kyrie said softly. She wanted to reach out, to hug Medusa and try to make everything that was happening to her okay. But she knew she couldn't. "Stheno will just have to bring your stuff there."

Medusa nodded.

"The truck's in the back alley. Leave your car here. Don't tell me where you're going. Then I don't have to lie if they show up here." Elijah grabbed Medusa's phone when she handed it over and repeated what he'd done to the previous one. "I'll send over the new files to your computer. Don't hook up to the motel wifi."

"I know, I know," Kyrie huffed.

"You owe me big for this one, Kyrie," he warned, stepping back from the bar to lead them to the back door.

"I'll make you a deal: next time you're accused of murder, I'll take your case." Kyrie laughed, shooting Elijah a wink. He just snorted and rolled his eyes. "What? It could happen."

"Whatever. Get out of here. I think they put out a BOLO on your plates."

"Fabulous. You know … I really liked that car."

"It was a piece of junk," Medusa drawled. Kyrie would have glared at her for the comment and told her that ol'Bessy was a good car who had served Kyrie well over the years, but she was just glad to hear Medusa sounding normal again.

The drive to the next motel, a shabby thing on the other side of Lore, was silent. Kyrie tapped her fingers against the steering wheel to work out some of the nervous energy that buzzed beneath her skin like static.

Medusa sat in the car while Kyrie booked them another room. The woman behind the front desk didn't even ask to see ID. She just popped her bubble gum and went back to watching her soap operas on the little TV behind the desk.

Kyrie drove around back, parking the truck right in front of their room, with the rail end facing the building. They spent the next few minutes unloading the noodles, Kyrie's go-bag, and the completed noodle sculptures that Elijah had helpfully sat on a board.

"Home sweet home." Medusa scowled, looking at the single queen bed, then flopping down on it and staring up at the dingy ceiling. "Tell me why we can't get a penthouse or something in all this? Or at the very least a normal hotel room? Doesn't even have to have three stars."

"Because those places check ID, and they want credit cards that they can charge for room service, and mini bars, and other expenses." Kyrie slid the board with her noodle art carefully onto the little round table in the corner. The linguine skyscraper wobbled a little but stayed standing.

"Right."

"I'm sorry you're uncomfortable." Kyrie worried her lip. She moved around the little crime scenes, needing something to stay her hands.

"Don't apologize for things that aren't your fault."

Kyrie nodded, smiling a little to herself. "Well, at least we got one thing from this."

"What?" Medusa had rolled onto her side, one pillow tucked under her chin like a teddy bear as she eyed Kyrie.

"We know you aren't the killer." Kyrie gave her a cheeky grin.

Medusa growled and threw the pillow at her, nearly taking out the little Stone & Son's Excavation replica

"Oi! Watch the art!" Kyrie laughed. "I'm going to grab us some snacks from the gas station down the street. You call Stheno and tell her you'll meet her around the block, then you can have the first shower."

"Yeah. Thanks." Medusa sat up to catch the new burner Kyrie threw at her.

The shower was still going when Kyrie got back. Stheno had been and gone, leaving a duffle on the end of the bed for Medusa. Medusa was singing some old pop song in the shower, her voice deep and smooth, with the door propped open a crack to let out the steam. Kyrie shook her head and dropped onto the bed with an unopened bottle of Fanta and the laptop.

She'd finished half the bottle of garishly orange soda by

the time Medusa came out in a loose pair of sweatpants and Kyrie's hoodie, with a towel wrapped around her hair.

"Is that the file on the latest murder?"

"Yeah." Kyrie grabbed the soda bottle and set it onto the floor before patting the bed beside her. "They found something interesting at the scene."

"Don't tell me. More green hair." Medusa flopped beside her with a huff. Kyrie forced herself, with some difficulty, not to notice how warm Medusa's leg was pressed against her own.

Instead, she scrolled down to the pictures so Medusa could look at them. "The latest victim was clutching this in her hand."

"That's Athena's amulet." Medusa's voice had gone soft. She leaned in closer to get a better look at the picture, her towel bumping Kyrie in the nose. "Sorry."

"You're good."

Medusa nodded, leaning back against the headboard. "So whoever it was, they were wearing one of Athena's amulets."

"That's what it looks like."

"That means …"

"That it's one of Athena's priestesses, her higher ups in the company. Which makes a lot of sense, all things considered. It had to be someone with intimate knowledge of your case, and easy access to you. So … who in Athena's order has a grudge against you?"

"No one." Medusa shrugged helplessly. "That I know of."

"*Someone* must."

CHAPTER 10

After a full twenty-four hours of being cooped up in the room together, Kyrie looked up from her latest noodle crime scene to say, "We should get out of here for a bit."

"And go where?" Medusa asked, not looking up from the book that Stheno had thrown in her bag. It was one of those ridiculous cozy mysteries that she and her sisters read together. She'd been a quarter of the way through it when all hell had broken loose in her life.

"Out to dinner."

Medusa sighed. She tucked an old receipt she'd found in the bottom of her duffle into the book, then turned to give Kyrie her full attention. At least until she shot her down.

"I don't think that's a good idea," Medusa said.

"Why not?"

"Oh. I don't know. Because I'm wanted for murder, and you're wanted for accessory, and there is a murderer out there who probably wants both of us dead? Take your pick." Medusa wasn't sure why Kyrie was suggesting it. It seemed like a silly, frivolous thing. They didn't need to go out. Medusa had her book. Kyrie had her noodles. They were fine.

"I won't let anything bad happen to you," Kyrie pressed, her brows drawing together in seriousness. "You trust me. Don't you?"

"It's not about that …"

"Look, we need to unwind a little. This situation is stressful enough without being stuck in a two-by-two room together for twenty-four hours. It'll only be worse if we let this whole thing make us feel trapped."

§

In the end, Kyrie won out, and Medusa found herself at a little restaurant around the corner from their motel. It was an Italian place. The smell of garlic lingered heavily in the air. Kyrie had gotten them a table in the back corner, out of the way, and Medusa sat the whole time with her hood over her hair.

"I don't think I'll ever look at pasta the same way," Medusa muttered, stabbing a piece of gnocchi pointedly.

"Sorry?" Kyrie laughed.

"No, you're not," Medusa grumped, taking another mouthful of pasta.

"No, I'm not," Kyrie agreed.

"How did you figure out the noodle thing worked for you, anyway? It seems like such an off-the-wall way of thinking."

"I had a teacher in college who gave us this mixed-media project. We had to explain a concept of psychology with art." Kyrie twirled her fork to scoop up some of the spaghetti on her plate. "The trick was—"

"Using art to explain psychology concepts wasn't the trick?" That sounded like the trick to Medusa, at least.

"No." Kyrie laughed, a lock of hair slithering out of the loose braid on her shoulder as she shook her head. "The trick was doing it on a college student's budget. If you weren't an art student, you didn't already have art supplies, and those things get expensive. A lot of kids just went out and got a box of crayons from the dollar store, but I don't know … that just seemed to easy."

"You like a challenge."

"As much as I appreciate your running commentary, can I finish my story?" Kyrie quirked a brow. Her words may have been scolding, but her lips twitched up into a teasing grin.

Medusa nodded.

"Plus, noodles have a dual purpose. Whatever I didn't use for the project, I could eat."

"Very sensible."

"I thought so." Kyrie's grin widened. Her eyes were laughing, even if her mouth wasn't, and Medusa found she couldn't quite look away. Nor was she sure that she wanted to. "Anyway. I got the highest grade out of the whole class! My professor asked to keep my project as an example for when she taught it again the following semester."

"What was your concept?"

"You know … I don't even remember."

Medusa snorted.

"What? I can't be expected to remember everything! That was like … eight years ago?"

"You've got no idea?" Medusa teased.

"No, I can't remember exactly what semester I took it." Kyrie sat back in her chair, pouting. "You're laughing at me."

"I am." Medusa snickered, and that was that. The rest of dinner was gentle prodding and teasing. Medusa ignored the little voice in her head that whispered something about flirting. That wasn't what this was.

"I've been thinking," Medusa said, breaking the silence of their walk back to their room.

"That sounds dangerous."

Medusa bumped Kyrie lightly with her shoulder. "Shut up and listen."

"I am listening."

"I want my original file, from when the original Perseus found me." Medusa kept her voice low, carefully neutral, worried that if she got too loud, Kyrie might hear how nervous she was at the thought.

"You think whoever is doing this now had something to do with the original attack."

Medusa breathed slowly, forcing her face to remain blank. She didn't look over at Kyrie, but she could feel her watching, analyzing, seeing things that Medusa hadn't ever wanted another person to see.

"Elijah can get his hands on those," Kyrie said, not waiting for Medusa to confirm nor deny her suspicions. It didn't seem to matter much to Kyrie what Medusa's reasoning was. "I'll give him a call when we get back to the room."

"Thanks."

"No problem." Kyrie pulled out the key card from her pocket and swiped it in the door. She pushed it open with a soft creak of unoiled hinges, then stopped dead on the threshold.

"Kyrie, get out of the way. I want to sleep off all of this pasta."

"We have to go." Kyrie grabbed Medusa's hand and tugged. But Medusa was quick. She took a step into the room just as Kyrie spun out of the way, and got an eyeful of what had stopped Kyrie.

The smell was the first thing she noticed, all raw and metallic. The next were the noodles everywhere, covered in a gooey red substance that had made them soft. Medusa couldn't place it right away. But when her eyes fell to the body on the bed, *their* bed, it all sunk in.

She felt her stomach twist, sharp and violent, the gnocchi from dinner making a bid for freedom from her throat.

"We have to go, Medusa." Kyrie sounded panicked now, but her voice was somewhere far off. Like Medusa was underwater, sinking to the bottom of an ocean of crimson viscera. "Medusa! We have to *GO!*"

Medusa felt herself being pulled, her arm jerking when Kyrie yanked her into a run just as the red and blue flashing lights of a squad car pulled up outside of their room.

CHAPTER 11

Kyrie dragged Medusa several blocks, until she was sure they had left the lights of Perseus in the distance and she could feel the frenzied panic calming in her veins.

The office to the next motel was lit by a dim yellow light. Which was good because Kyrie knew how they looked: harried and red from running. She didn't want anyone to ask questions. And the surest way to avoid that was …

"Hi," Kyrie giggled drunkenly, hooking her arm around the elbow of an unresponsive Medusa. "My wife and I are on our honeymoon. And we—"

"Room 357," the woman said disinterestedly, holding out a keycard. "That'll be eighty-nine dollars for the night."

"Oh, thank you!" Kyrie crooned cheerfully. She pulled out the emergency cash Elijah had stuffed into the glovebox of the truck and thanked the gods she'd thought to grab it. After a quick count, she handed the woman exact change and took the key.

Then she tugged Medusa along to their room.

"Why is it always one bed with you lately?" Medusa asked. Her tone was distant, blank. She was standing in the middle of the room, gaze far away as she took in her surroundings without really seeing them. She seemed to be surfacing slowly, but that was better than not at all.

"What?"

"I wish we could get a room with two beds for once." Medusa grumbled. Her gaze had fixed on the bed, eyes narrowed like it had kicked her cat.

Kyrie blinked at her for a minute, frowning, then she sighed. It had to be some kind of dissonance, a coping mechanism. Medusa was making a joke to keep their focus away from what they'd just seen. If that was the case, Kyrie would bite.

"But darling," she cooed as playfully as she could manage. Kyrie took a step from the door to stand next to Medusa, bumping shoulders with her. If this was what Medusa needed, to pretend what they'd seen hadn't happened, Kyrie would give her that. "We're on our honeymoon."

Medusa groaned, shoving Kyrie hard enough to send her stumbling into the dresser with an old TV propped on top of it. "We are not! Stop tell—Why would you tell people that?!"

Kyrie shrugged, going to the bathroom to check if they needed extra towels. They would both need to wash up, and probably wash their shoes. She didn't want to drag any of that mess around with them when they picked the next place. She toed off her Converse, dumped them in the bathtub, and then returned to sprawl onto the bed, staring up at the ceiling.

Medusa was still standing in the middle of the room, waiting for an answer.

"People are less likely to think it's weird that we don't leave our room much if they think we're on our honeymoon," she said simply.

"Oh." A faint redness settled into Medusa's cheeks.

"Plus, it makes you blush. Every. Time. It's cute." Kyrie shrugged, which when lying on her back on the bed just looked like a full body wiggle. "Take off your shoes and let's go put them in the tub."

"Why?"

"They might have blood on them."

Medusa dropped to the floor to untie her shoes and kick them off. "I'm tired."

"I know. You can sleep soon." Kyrie rolled off the bed to scoop up the sneakers. "Get in bed. I'll dump these in the bath and get them rinsed off."

Medusa didn't say anything. She just laid on her back in the middle of the dingy, rust-colored motel carpet. Her eyes were closed behind her glasses, the hood from Kyrie's hoodie falling back over her forehead. Kyrie sighed. She put the shoes in the tub to deal with later, leaving the light on, then bent to scoop Medusa up as best she could. With one arm around Medusa's shoulders and the other around her waist, Kyrie tugged her to her feet and helped her over to the bed.

Once Medusa was lying down, Kyrie struggled to get the covers from under her. There came the soft pop of stitches tugging loose, which she determinedly ignored, and then she pulled it up to Medusa's neck.

"Kyrie?" Medusa's voice was soft, only just loud enough to be heard above the sound of a truck driving past.

"Yeah?"

"When will this be over?"

"Soon. We'll figure it out soon." Kyrie wasn't sure she could actually deliver on that promise, but she was going to try.

"I'm so tired."

"I know you are. It's been a long couple of days." Kyrie knelt by the bed so she could whisper to Medusa without having to hunch.

"No. All of it. I'm tired of all of it." There was sniffle from somewhere in the depths of Medusa's hood, but Kyrie was not going to mention that.

Kyrie sighed. "Get some sleep. I'll be back in a minute. I need to rinse off our shoes."

"I don't know why."

"I don't either, Medusa. But we'll figure it out, and whoever it is will be punished for what they've done to you." Kyrie looked over her shoulder at the bathroom. The light was still on, their shoes already in the tub. She shook her head. "Scoot over. I'm getting in there with you."

Medusa shuffled closer to the center of the bed, leaving Kyrie just enough room to perch herself on the edge. But it was enough. Kyrie took one of the hands that Medusa had curled up in her sleeves and squeezed it between her own.

"What did I do wrong?" Medusa asked after a few moments of shaking breaths.

"Oh, honey. Nothing. You didn't do anything. This was done *to* you, not the other way around." Kyrie reached up to brush the hood back from Medusa's face so she could see her eyes behind the lenses of her glasses. "You didn't ask for this, and nothing you did made you deserving of it. Do you understand me?"

Medusa nodded, but she didn't look sure. Kyrie couldn't see the tears, but she heard another loud sniffle. "I think someone told Poseidon where to find me all those years ago."

"That cuts down our suspect pool a little. It should make things easier. But we'll think about that in the morning, okay?"

"I'm so tired," Medusa said again.

"Come here." Kyrie took Medusa by the upper arms and pulled her in close, pressing Medusa's face into her shoulder. With her arms wrapped around Medusa, she could feel the little hitches in the other woman's breath as she sobbed quietly. Kyrie rubbed slow circles into her back. "Shhh. Get some sleep. We're going to figure this out in the morning."

"What if they find us?"

"Then I'll chuck that huge ass remote at them," Kyrie said pointing to the remote for the TV. It was huge by remote standards, and probably heavier than the bible in the drawer below it. "I'm sure it'll knock them out."

Medusa laughed wetly against Kyrie's shoulder.

"You don't need to worry. I won't let anything happen to you." That was a promise she could keep. And Kyrie was happy to have made it when she felt the tension bleed out of Medua's shoulders, and her breath even out a moment later as she drifted off to sleep.

CHAPTER 12

SOMETHING HAD WOKEN HER. Medusa wasn't sure what. She'd fallen asleep easily, pressed into the warmth of Kyrie's arms. There was a safety there she hadn't felt in so very long that she tried not to think too hard about. Kyrie was, by her nature, off limits in Medusa's mind. Though in the hazy darkness of half-sleep, she wasn't sure why anymore.

Medusa's hand swiped out over the rough sheets, groping in the dark. The space where Kyrie had been had gone cold.

She blinked open her eyes to glare at the bathroom door. It was cracked open, a streak of light coming out from where it didn't quite meet the frame, glaring into her eyes.

"Kyrie?" Medusa croaked, rubbing her eyes under her glasses. The water was running in the bathroom. Maybe it was the shower? She couldn't tell. She groaned, pulling the covers over her face and rolling back over. She drifted for a while in that strange place between sleep and wakefulness, the place where she could still hear the water, but her mind supplied a waterfall instead of shower, painting a scene for her. An inlet with a waterfall, and lush greenery surrounding it. A peaceful place that she was sure she'd never been to, or if she had, it had been lifetimes ago.

The next time she came to was when a car alarm went off somewhere in the distance. It wasn't close enough to be in the parking lot, but maybe across the street? Lifting her head from the pillow, the first thing Medusa noticed was that the shower was still running, the door still opened just a crack as it'd been before.

"Kyrie?" Her words bounced off the walls, filling the silence with something other than running water, but there was no response. Adjusting her glasses, which had gone crooked in her sleep, she sat up. The red numbers of an alarm clock glared at her from the nightstand: 6:00 a.m.

Something wasn't right. She could feel it like a chill settling over the whole room.

"Kyrie." There would be no answer, she knew that. But she had to try. Medusa pulled herself to her feet, her steps sluggish against the carpet as she reached for the bathroom door. The plywood was rough beneath her fingers, and she held her breath, afraid of what she'd find on the other side.

It creaked loudly on the hinges, drowning out the sound of water on the other side for a moment. The sink was running, the washbasin pale yellow in the dim light but for a pool of dried red against the corner where it looked like someone had hit their head.

Medusa reached over to turn off the tap. Her eyes followed the blood down to a little pool gathered at the base of the sink. Then to a couple of drops that led toward the door. They disappeared after that, blending in with the garish colors of the motel carpeting, which hadn't been replaced since the '60s. Turning back to the bathroom, she grabbed her shoes from the tub and pulled them on just in time to hear the sirens outside.

"Shit," she hissed.

Red and blue flashed outside the window.

"Options. Options. Options," she muttered, blinking

around the tiny room. There weren't really any exits besides the door. Well. There was a tiny window in the bathroom over the tub. She glanced at it, judging whether she could fit through the space, and decided against it.

Medusa moved to the front window to draw back the curtains. The Perseus agents had gone into the little office downstairs.

Please, Athena, give me enough time," she prayed, and ducked out of the door. Slipping down the steps and around the corner without being seen was the work of a few minutes. And then she was trudging down a dark alley that smelled of garbage and something rancid. Once she was out of sight, Medusa took a deep breath, bracing herself on her knees. "All right, first things first. I've got to get in touch with Elijah."

Keeping to the back alleys of Lore, Medusa picked her way across the city to the black painted building that housed Elijah's bar. When she tugged on the front door and found it locked, she went around back. The knob jiggled in her hand, but the door didn't give.

"I'm sorry, Elijah," she muttered and grabbed a brick which clearly had been aside to hold the door open in the case of deliveries. A couple good hits, and the knob clattered to the ground, the door popping open. She pulled it closed, praying it would stay that way, and that Elijah didn't have an alarm system. He probably had an alarm system.

§

When Elijah arrived forty-five minutes later, Medusa had curled up in the chair in his back office.

"You're lucky I have cameras," he said flicking on the lights. "Otherwise, the police would be here."

"Yeah … lucky." Medusa shrugged, tugging the sleeves of Kyrie's hoodie down farther over her hands.

"Where's Kyrie?"

"They took her."

"Perseus?"

"No. Whoever …" Medusa swallowed, throat sharp and grating like sandpaper with emotion and disuse. "Whoever killed the others."

"Shit." Elijah ran a hand over his face, catching at his lower lip and letting it go against his teeth with a soft plop. "And you two hadn't figured out who that was yet."

It wasn't a question, but Medusa shook her head. "She was going to ask you for my original file."

"All right, let's get to work then. We don't have much time. I doubt whoever it is will hold Kyrie long before they're tired of her mouth. Out of the way." Elijah shooed her out of his chair and dropped in behind his computer. Fast fingers pecked away at the keyboard, pulling up a home screen with "The Liber Pater" in a scrolling font as the background. A couple more clicks led to another interface with a plain black screen, and the word "Oracle" in a gray so close to the black that she almost missed it.

"What the hell is that?"

"Don't worry your pretty little head about it, sweetie," Elijah muttered. "Go grab me a coffee?"

Medusa glared at him, baring her teeth.

"Trust me, it's a whole bunch of technical bullshit that I don't even understand half the time. Just let a man work!"

"Fine." Medusa huffed and headed to the kitchen to pour them both a cup of day-old stale coffee.

CHAPTER 13

Everything hurt.

Everything hurt and her gun was missing.

Why did everything hurt? Kyrie couldn't think past the dull ringing in her ears. Her brain told her arm to move, but the skin of her wrist met resistance against a coarse rope and remained stubbornly immobile.

"The hell happened?" she groaned, leaning her head back and staring up at the pitch-black ceiling.

Memories came back to her in flashes. She'd gotten up from the bed to brush her teeth, or at least scrub them with one of the towels since they hadn't had time to grab any of their things before fleeing. Kyrie ran her tongue over them. Nope. Still fuzzy. So she hadn't had time to even accomplish that much before the bathroom door creaked behind her.

In the dim light of the bathroom, there had been a face in the mirror. A face she recognized but couldn't place. The features had been familiar, but in a distant, distorted way. Then she was shoved. The world upended, spiraling. There was a distant crack, sharp pain bursting forth behind her closed eyelids.

And then …

And then ...

And then she was here. Tied to a chair. In the basement of ... some place.

"Hello?" Kyrie called.

Her voice echoing off the cement was the only response.

"All right. Don't panic. Medusa knows you're gone. She and Elijah will find you." Kyrie closed her eyes, inhaled a calming breath, and let it wash through her. All she had to do was wait.

"Wait, and stay awake," she reminded herself.

Her eyes began to droop almost as soon as she'd said those words. The concussion clearly wasn't going to make that easy on her. Her head jerked forward, and she pulled it upright again.

"Awake," she snorted to herself. "Never thought that would be this difficult."

The darkness pressed in on her, making it hard to focus on anything outside of the aches in her body, the ringing in her ears, and the cold oozing of blood down her neck.

"It's going to be a long night, Kyrie."

CHAPTER 14

THE PRINTER MADE a horrible racket as it spit out page after page of Medusa's original file written by Perseus himself. Perseus, it seemed, was particularly flowery in his language; all of his original files could have been novels for how long they were.

"I guess he wanted to make sure he got the details right?" Elijah asked, stapling a packet of pages together to make them easier to handle.

"Yeah." Medusa sipped from the cold mug of coffee at her side on the floor. It was taking all of her willpower not to rip apart every sheet of paper the noisy printer spit out. She didn't want to sit there and relive all of it. She did not want to think about everything that had happened. But ...

"Hey," Elijah said, reaching over to pat her shoulder awkward. "It's this or ..."

"Yeah, I know. It's this or we wait for Kyrie's body to turn up and hope there are enough clues on it to find the person. That's a non-option." Medusa wasn't sure when she had decided that exactly. She knew it wasn't just because she didn't want to be responsible for another person's death. There was something more to it than that. She shook the thought side. Now wasn't the time to dwell on things. Now was the time to dive headfirst into what happened to her all those years ago and hope it didn't swallow her whole.

She flipped through the latest packet Elijah had handed her, letting it dredge up images of the trial. Her sisters had been so supportive. Especially Stheno, who had held her hand through Poseidon's entire testimony. Medusa remembered it. All of it was burned into her brain like a picture on film.

The courtroom had smelled of sulfur, earth, and lightning from the gathering gods around them. Shteno and Euryale's shoulders were boney, and hurt where they dug into Medusa's on either side, but she didn't wish to be anywhere other than squeezed between them.

"It's not what it looked like," Poseidon had tried to argue. His eyes kept drifting to Medusa and her sisters, something in them begging. Medusa had found that odd at the time. What could he possibly have been asking her for? Surely he didn't think she'd call the whole thing off. Every time he looked their direction, Stheno and Euryale would squeeze her hands more tightly.

"She invited me," had been his final statement. But he couldn't provide any proof that she'd done any such thing. And Medusa hadn't. Why would she invite another god to Athena's temple? It wasn't that it was forbidden, but she'd never seen much reason to associate with the others. Athena provided for everything she needed. Or at least Athena had … before.

Medusa swallowed thickly, pushing the packet of papers away before the ink could smear with tears. She ran the sleeves of the hoodie underneath her lenses, and then grabbed the next packet.

"These are all from the end. I want the beginning. Where's the beginning?" She picked up another little stack, looked at the front page, and set it aside. "I want Perseus's account of how he found out the truth."

"It's coming. The damn thing prints backwards." Elijah grabbed more paper from the printer, rearranging it and stapling it together.

"Well that's stupid." Medusa huffed, grabbing the packet from him. The accounts from Athena were sparse. Mostly just that Athena had discovered her temple desecrated after Medusa fled and reacted in rage. Medusa had blamed Athena for that for a long time. The fury Athena had turned on her, the curse she couldn't remove once cast, it hadn't been fair. To turn to stone any living creature she laid eyes on … But Athena had apologized in the only way a god could: she'd given Medusa anything she'd asked for. The thing was, Medusa had never asked for much. A job. A home. A cat.

"Why didn't you?" Elijah asked, voicing the question Medusa had asked herself countless times before. "You could have asked Athena for anything, and you didn't."

"The one thing I wanted, she couldn't give me. Even gods can't change history. It was a fixed point. It changed the tide. Even if she could have gone back and saved me, I wouldn't have asked her to. She could have erased the events, but the … the *feeling* would still have been here." She tapped her temple. "It would never truly go away." Medusa shrugged, flipping through pages of black ink on white paper and not really seeing the words. Did she honestly need them? The events were still there, etched into the back of her mind. Engraving on stone. Maybe she'd missed something. Maybe Perseus had seen something she hadn't. "Wait. This says someone reported it to Athena. She didn't just stumble upon the scene."

"What?" Elijah leaned in to look at the paper upside down. When that didn't work, he scooted across the floor to sit beside her and read over her shoulder. "Huh. Let me see if they have record of the original report."

Elijah dug through the packets of paper, a frown creasing his wrinkle-free forehead. Medusa set about bringing some order to the papers in front of her. Notes on the trial were set aside.

"Ah ha! Victory is mine!" Elijah crowed, brandishing a stack of papers as if he'd won a prize. He ducked his head to flip through the pages, mouth moving as he read. "Huh. That's weird."

"What?"

"They redacted the name."

"Well, un-redact it." Medusa huffed, snatching the pages from his hands.

"Awwww," Elijah cooed, tilting his head and clutching his heart. "That's cute."

"What?"

"You think I'm some all-powerful technology god. But if it was redacted centuries ago, it's gone, sweetie."

"Tch." Medusa clicked her tongue, rolling her eyes. "Is that the report? Hand it over."

"Why? It's not like—"

She snatched it from his fingers.

"Grabby! Grabby! So rude! Where are your manners?"

Medusa wasn't listening anymore. Her eyes were scanning the written transcript of whoever had told Athena. Something niggled at the back of her mind. Something familiar. This was ... she knew this person.

"What is it?"

"Do we have the transcripts of my sisters' testimonies?"

"Yeah, I think they're still printing." Elijah grabbed the pile and started digging. "Why? What do you see?"

"I'm not sure yet." Medusa shook her head. "And grab me Poseidon's testimony from that pile over there."

CHAPTER 15

KEEPING herself conscious was proving harder than Kyrie would have liked. Normally, she suffered from a low-level insomnia, and being tied to a chair as she was would have made it impossible to sleep. But it was so dark, and cold. Add to that the dizziness that was settling in. Was it dizziness? It was hard to tell with the blackness around her.

How long had it been?

How long had she been out this time?

There were no windows. Something chemical lingered in the air, maybe from cleaning supplies? She couldn't place the smell. But it wasn't entirely quiet like she'd originally thought. There were footsteps somewhere off in the distance. Maybe if she shouted loud enough, someone would hear her.

Or maybe it would just alert her captor to the fact that she was awake.

That might be a bad idea, Kyrie, she thought, shaking her head. Whoever had killed those other Perseus agents hadn't exactly gone for the quickest methods. They'd made sure their victims suffered. The longer it took for her captor to realize she was awake, the longer she'd likely stay alive.

Now, if only she knew how long it had been since she'd been taken. Or who had taken her.

Kyrie closed her eyes and tried to picture the face again. It was still fuzzy from the ache in her head and the darkness of the motel bathroom. But there was something about it. Something she had placed immediately. The slope of the woman's nose. The shape of her eyes that reminded Kyrie of … They reminded her of …

The darkness was pressing in again at the edges of her memory. It was all going hazy.

"No," she gasped, trying to hold on to the image. But it was already slipping away along with everything else. Her lids fluttered closed. She pulled them open, fought against the pull to cling to the waking world. But it was too late. She was being dragged under again. Down. Down. To sleep.

CHAPTER 16

Medusa's eyes sped across the page. She'd read the same testimony three times, the report another five. They were undeniably from the same person. It wasn't an exact science, and Medusa was by no means a linguist, but she recognized her sister in the report.

"This is Euryale," she announced handing Elijah the two sheets of paper.

"How do you know?" Elijah looked down at the paper with raised brows. "I don't see how you can tell."

"She's my sister." Medusa eyed him blandly. "That's Euryale. The question is, *why* is it Euryale?"

"Let's look at your sisters' records. I didn't look up how they were doing." Elijah shot to his feet, scattering papers in his rush to reach the desk chair. He threaded his fingers together and pushed them over his head, cracking the knuckles. The groan he let out when he lowered his arms again was theatrical, dramatic. Medusa rolled her eyes.

"We don't have all sorts of time for pomp."

"There is always time for pomp," Elijah said with a wink over his shoulder.

Medusa moved to lean against the back of his chair,

squinting at the screen. His fingers were typing away in seconds, flying across the keyboard at a rate that didn't quite seem human. Medusa shook her head and pushed that thought aside for another time.

"Euryale got married a few decades ago," she supplied. "She has kids and everything. I don't think she had anything to do with this. It's Stheno we need to look into."

Elijah nodded. He typed Stheno's name into the search bar, clicked Enter, and sat back as the screen filled with information.

Medusa pushed her glasses further up her nose and leaned in closer to get a better look. There were property and employment records, along with financial statements.

"This is all too current. I need further back. Closer to when it all happened. Is there any way to get those?"

"Can you be more specific? That stuff will be harder to hunt down. Maybe if I knew exactly what you were looking for …" Elijah grabbed the mouse to click through the records he'd pulled up. He closed out anything more recent.

"Who got my temple?"

"What?"

"When I left Athena's service, who got my temple? Who took my place as one of her high priestesses?"

"Didn't your sisters already have their own temples?" Elijah frowned, but the mouse was still clicking, digging further and further back. As some point, they'd switched from English to Greek.

"They did. But mine overlooked the sea. High priestesses got first pick whenever a new temple was erected, and I wanted that one. Lots of us did." Medusa shrugged. "It was one of the most beautiful temples the humans had ever built for Athena."

It had been. She remembered that much. All shining white granite and sea salt air. It sparkled in the sunshine and shone in the moonlight. Its roof hardly ever saw any rain. And then there was the library. The shelves upon shelves of ancient literature, and future literature, and everything in between that Athena had ferreted away beneath the temple floor. Medusa had spent hours upon hours just reading. Keeping the temple up to par wasn't hard, as so many of the humans in that area were devout followers. They respected the temple as much as she did, and wanted to keep it beautiful, which left her plenty of free time.

"Oh," Elijah said, drawing her from her memories.

"What is it?"

"Stheno was given your place on the high priestess council, and your temple." Elijah pointed to the screen, finger hovering but not touching the glass. "She took possession five days after you'd been banished."

"Of course she did." Medusa sagged against the chair, her own weight too much to hold up all of the sudden. "My foolish baby sister."

"But if Euryale was the one who set it all up, why would Stheno reap the rewards?" Elijah's eyes scanned the documents in front of him. "It doesn't make sense."

"Because Euryale didn't set it up." Medusa was sure of that.

"But—"

"She was the eldest, but the high priestess life isn't what she wanted. She wanted something simpler. She only went into service for Athena because that's what was expected of all of us." Medusa's fingers tapped against the hard back of the chair, her mind working over all of the information. "Once she'd done her years, she left the service entirely and started a family. That's what she'd always wanted."

"Then why tell Athena about what happened?"

"Because our darling golden child, with the adorable smile and the big eyes, our baby sister, asked her to. Oh,

Stheno. What have you done?" She sighed heavily. Then her mind flashed to a receipt crumpled in the bottom of her bag. The address had been a gas station near one of the crime scenes. She hadn't thought anything of it at the time. Except … Medusa didn't drive. She had no use for gas. But Stheno did. She had a nice car that always looked like it had just been detailed. "I need a car, and I need addresses for anywhere Stheno could be holding Kyrie."

"She has a lot of holdings. You're going to have to narrow it down for me," Elijah said, fingers already typing in search terms and coming up with addresses.

"Get me a map."

"What? Why?"

"A map. Print me out a map. And the addresses of the crime scenes."

Elijah nodded. At some point while they were speaking, the printer had finished printing pages from her file; they were covering the floor. It now spat out a black and white map, and Medusa grabbed a pen from the desk to mark locations.

"What is it? What do you see?" Elijah leaned into her light, and she swatted him back so she could see better.

"Stheno's got a nice car. She wouldn't park it just anywhere. It might get towed, or dinged, or broken into."

"Okay?"

"She had to be able to walk to the crime scenes from her main office. Which means the building she works out of is this little circle." Medusa connected every crime scene like dots.

"Couldn't she have taken a cab, or called for a driver or something?"

"There would be a paper trail. Stheno wouldn't want a paper trail. She's too meticulous for all that. We read murder mysteries together. She always said she'd be able to plan the perfect murder." Medusa snorted. "Get me any addresses she owns in this circle."

"Wow. Medusa and her sisters have a murder mystery book club. Add that to the list of things I didn't know I needed in my life." Elijah laughed.

"Elijah. The addresses."

"Right!" He grabbed the map and moved back to the computer. After a few clicks, and some soft muttering, he nodded. "Looks like she rents office space out of this building. A whole floor."

Medusa narrowed her eyes where the cursor had landed, then grabbed his keys.

She was halfway out of the door when she heard Elijah shout, "Wait! I'm coming with!"

CHAPTER 17

THE NEXT TIME Kyrie came to, it was to the sound of rushing traffic unmuffled by a building and the burn of the late evening sun on her eyelids. She was outside. Or close to an open window. Peeking her eyes open just a crack, hoping no one would notice, she saw that it was in fact a window. A big office window overlooking a full parking lot.

"Ah. You're awake," a voice said over her shoulder. It shook with laughter.

"This doesn't fit your usual motif, does it?" Kyrie asked, not bothering to try turning to see who the voice belonged to. It didn't matter. There wasn't time to worry about that. She needed to figure out how to get out of the chair and away from whoever it was.

"Sadly, no. There is no quarry, or cement, or excavation company nearby. It's a pity, really, I thought that was rather clever." The voice sighed.

"Yeah. Clever." Kyrie snorted.

"You didn't think so?" The voice sounded like it was pouting.

"Seemed a bit pedestrian is all. A little on the nose." Kyrie shrugged. "You get the whole thing off some show?"

"Not that it really matters," the voice went on as if Kyrie hadn't spoken at all. "This will be the last. We just have to wait for my darling sister to get here."

"Sister." Kyrie mouthed the word to herself. That's why the face looked so familiar. It reminded her of Medusa.

"Medusa will be here very soon, I imagine. She always did figure out who the killer was in our book club before I did." The voice—no, Stheno sounded like she was pouting again. As if Medusa was ruining all her fun.

"Then all of it—Poseidon, Athena's curse—it was all ..."

"Yes, yes, you're very clever. But it took you much too long to figure it all out. I had thought the first time I killed near your motel, that would have been it. It was so *obvious*. But I guess you and Medusa just weren't as smart as you thought you were." Stheno came around to sit on the ledge of the window, her hand bracketing her hips. "Maybe if I hadn't destroyed all your cute little macaroni towers, you'd have figured it out quicker." She winked.

"Why do you think Medusa is coming here?" Kyrie wiggled her wrists carefully, trying to loosen the bindings without Stheno noticing.

"Oh, because I left her all the clues, of course. I expect she'll be here in about ... ten minutes? Let's make it a game, shall we? You guess a time and whoever is closest wins."

"What do I get if I win? Do I get to live?"

Stheno laughed, a bell-like laugh that would have been more fitting from a wood nymph. "Oh gosh no. But it's cute that you think that would work. Also, don't bother with the ropes. I'll let you out soon enough. You have to jump, after all."

"I'm not going to jump," Kyrie said through clenched teeth.

"Oh child, I didn't say you were going to jump willingly, just that you'd jump. No. Medusa will be here, of course. And it'll look like she pushed you. I'll be devastated. My poor wonderful older sister, middle child, all of that pressure." She shook her head, tsk-ing lightly. "It just got to be too much, and she snapped."

"She's not coming. She doesn't know where I am. And if she did know, she wouldn't come here. She's not that stupid."

Stheno leaned out the window a little, her hands still braced on the sill to keep herself from falling. She looked down at the cars in the lot, a spark of delight twisting her features.

"Isn't that her? And look, she brought a friend! Oh goodie! A double murder!" Stheno fell forward toward her feet, clapping happily. "Well, it looks like I won. You said never, I said ten minutes. I was much closer."

She reached into the desk behind Kyrie, pulling out a gun. A terribly familiar gun. Kyrie's eyes widened.

"Perseus was smart, wasn't he? To harness the power of the Gorgon in a single bullet. All one needs to do is take aim, and fire, and the bullet will do the work of Medusa's stare. It really came in handy for you all, I'm sure. But it's a shame you didn't keep better track of your sidearm." She shook her head, clicking her tongue. "Ah well."

CHAPTER 18

"You should stay here," Medusa said, reaching for the car door.

Elijah jabbed the lock button before she could get out. "Kyrie is my best friend."

"I know that. But another mortal up there is just going to be another moving target for Stheno, and trust me, she's good at hitting a moving target. You stay down here and call reinforcements."

"Who am I supposed to call? The only people who know you're not the killer is us!"

Medusa sighed, bumping her head back against the headrest. "That's why you're going to call Perseus and you're going to tell them where I am."

"What? That's—"

"Tell them I took Kyrie hostage, and I've gone to confront my sister about some petty grievance. They'll show up with a whole fleet of highly trained agents ready to do anything they can to save Kyrie."

"And you?"

Medusa shrugged. It didn't matter. She'd made up her

mind about that. What happened to her, happened to her. So long as Kyrie got out.

"You absolute moron." Elijah heaved a heavy breath, blowing the artfully cut bangs off his forehead. Then he leaned backward to grab two phones from the back seat. "That's a stupid plan. Here's what we're going to do instead."

"Elijah—"

"Here's what we're going to do instead!" he growled, thrusting one of the phones at her. He dialed one of them with the other. "Keep this line open. Mute it, stuff it into your hoodie pocket, and keep it open."

"Then what?"

"Get Stheno talking. You're her sister, that shouldn't be too hard. You let me worry about the rest."

Medusa narrowed her eyes at him, staring hard for a long minute, then nodded. "I'm trusting you."

"And I'm trusting you. So we're even. Now, go get our Kyrie back."

"Should we, like … hug. Or something?" Medusa asked, shifting uncomfortably in her seat.

"Not necessary."

"Good." Medusa nodded and climbed out of the car. As she shut the door, she heard the dial tone of another phone.

"Perseus Initiative," a bored sounding operator answered.

"Hello. This … oh my gods … this is … Medusa took me hostage and made me drive her to …" Elijah whimpered dramatically into the phone.

Medusa cocked her head at him through the window. He smiled and held up two thumbs. She rolled her eyes, then headed into the building. The elevator boasted a convenient menu of the businesses inside, and it was easy enough to find Stheno's floor labeled simply with her name. The office was surprisingly empty when Medusa stepped off the elevator. She frowned, looking around. There were plenty of desks, each with the personal touches of someone who worked there five days a week, but no one sat in the chairs.

"She's expecting me." That maybe should have put Medusa on edge, but it didn't. Instead, she felt calm settle into her muscles. "Of course she's expecting me."

She padded slowly across the wood-floored office space, toward where Stheno's door was propped open. She didn't try to be quiet or sneaky. What point would there have been?

"Oh look! She's finally shown up!" Stheno crowed. She was sitting on the edge of her desk, her arms crossed over her chest. Medusa's eyes flicked over her, to the chair where Kyrie was tied facing the window, then down to the heavy looking pistol on the desk.

"Is that Kyrie's?"

Stheno shrugged. "I don't think she'll be needing it anymore. Am I right, Kyrie?"

"Is that the game here? Make it look like she shot me in self-defense?" Medusa moved to lean against the doorframe, casual. "How you doing over there, Kyrie?"

"Just peachy, darling," Kyrie called back over her shoulder. "Neck's a bit stiff, but I'm sure we can sort that out later."

"Flirt," Medusa scoffed fondly. "So, Stheno, how is this going to go? You know I could end this pretty quick. All I'd have to do is take off my glasses and turn you to stone."

"Ah, but I might duck. You might miss and hit our dear miss Alcides back there." Stheno shook her head smiling. "All you have to do is look at a living thing unobstructed, and it turns to stone, right? You wouldn't want to risk that, would you? Plus, who's to say I wouldn't get a shot off before you did." Stheno looked entirely relaxed, a wide, playful smile splitting her lips. "No. You pushed miss Alcides out the window, you see. And me? Oh, me. I tried to stop you. I grabbed her gun and was able to fire off a single shot just as Miss Alcides fell to her untimely death. Poor thing."

"That's it then?"

"It's a little simple for my tastes." Stheno shrugged. "But needs must."

Medusa sighed, her shoulder slumping.

"What?" Shteno's face twisted into disappointment. "Tired, big sister?"

"I'm just wondering what all this is for. I mean, you've got everything, don't you? Everything I was going to have. Why bother with all this—the murders, the framing, Poseidon —nastiness?"

Stheno rose from her perch on the desk, leaving the gun behind, seemingly at ease with her position of power, and began to pace in between it and the two chairs in front. Her hands didn't shake, but Medusa saw the hard set of her shoulders, the rage lining her spine.

"Athena always liked you better," Stheno said like it was the most obvious thing in the world.

"Jealousy, then?" Medusa snorted and took a step into the office. She turned to look at the shelf along the wall; accolades and pictures lined it. All of Stheno's accomplishments. "You know what they say about jealousy, don't you sister?"

"What?" Stheno stopped pacing. The gun was between them on the corner of the desk. A couple of quick paces and Medusa could have her hands on it. She just had to be quick. But could she be quicker than Stheno?

"It'll turn you into a monster." Medusa's smile was all teeth.

Stheno threw her head back and laughed, the sound more mania than happiness. That's when Medusa saw the lights out of the corner of her eye. Perseus was here. They hadn't used the sirens, lest they alert their targets, but they were already presumably infiltrating the building.

Medusa lunged for her sister, taking her to the ground

hard. Stheno's green locs smacked against the floor, making her head bounce a little.

"You'd know all about monsters, wouldn't you, Medusa?" Stheno asked. She was still laughing as she grabbed for Medusa's throat, both hands tightening around it to cut off her breath. Medusa choked, sobbed, gasped around the hold, her own hands scrambling at Stheno's wrists, clawing at the skin to get them loose.

Stheno kicked out, rolling them so Medusa's head smacked against one of the chair legs. She could feel consciousness slipping away from her. But the roll had knocked her glasses loose. Instead of fighting to get free from Stheno's hold, she squeezed her eyes shut and tore them off.

Stheno let go, made to scramble away, but it was too late. Medusa opened her eyes just as her sister released her throat. The dead weight of stone teetered for a moment, and Medusa rolled out of the way before it thunked softly against the rug.

Medusa pushed herself onto her hands and knees, gasping for breath and scrambling for her glasses. She found them a moment later, pressing them back on her face with enough force to make her nose ache.

"You going to untie me now?" Kyrie asked from where she was still facing the window.

"Yeah. Give me a minute."

CHAPTER 19

WITH THE RECORDED confession Elijah was able to provide for Perseus, and all the evidence they'd acquired during their little stint in amateur detecting, Medusa was cleared of all charges. Knowing what had really happened to her all those centuries ago had lifted one weight but replaced it with another. Knowing that it had been the betrayal of a beloved sister left Medusa feeling not entirely whole anymore. And after that … well. She couldn't very well stay in Lore, could she?

Kyrie had come along, and though her reasons were her own, Medusa thought maybe it was all that lingered in the air of Lore. Turning what was once a shining city into something more tainted. Darker.

The air was crisp and cool when the beat-up old red sedan pulled up to the small bed and breakfast.

"We'll have to hire someone to handle those bushes. I don't do gardening," Medusa muttered, looking up at the cream siding and the wrap-around porch. She'd managed to put a down payment on it with what little savings she'd had from the coffee shop. A bed and breakfast—a business—all her own. It was worth it.

"I might be able to do that," Kyrie volunteered from the driver's seat.

"I saw your succulents."

"So?"

"You are not doing the gardening. Or making the coffee," Medusa said, climbing out of the car. "Nor will you be in charge of cleaning."

"Then what *can* I do?!" Kyrie slammed her door and came around to the trunk to help with the last of the boxes.

"I don't know. We'll find something for you. But you are not touching the garden or coffee."

"Oh, fine," Kyrie huffed. She looped her arm around Medusa's middle to pull her into a quick hug. Medusa stared up at the building again, looking a little lost. "What's up? Not regretting the move, are we? 'Cause I can probably get my job back if I—"

"Gods. Do you ever shut up?" Medusa chuckled, bumping Kyrie with her hip. "I was just thinking about Mythos. It's different. It reminds me of my temple a little."

"It does?"

"Yeah." Medusa nodded, closing her eyes to listen to a seagull caw as it flew over them. "It's nice. I like it."

THE END

ACKNOWLEDGMENTS

First off, thank you—the reader—for sticking with me as I wrote my first murder mystery, literally ever. I really appreciate it, and I hope you'll drop a review on GoodReads to let me know what you think.

I'm not sure yet if I'll be writing more about Medusa and Kyrie, or even if I'll dip into mystery again, it'll largely depend on how well received this story is. But keep an eye on my social media for future updates.

Next, I'd like the thank my small hoard of beta-readers. You guys gave some excellent insight, and I really appreciate all of your hard work. And my editor Meg for turning this into a story worth reading.

And last but certainly not least, thank you to my writing community. Particularly, Tiss, Elle, and Jasmine who I have known for near a decade now—without you there would be no Lou. And to my new friends, Candace, Melania, Nancy, Tanya, and Erin for being supportive and awesome.

ABOUT THE AUTHOR

Born and raised in a small town near the Chesapeake Bay, Lou Wilham grew up on a steady diet of fiction, arts and crafts, and Old Bay. After years of absorbing everything, there was to absorb of fiction, fantasy, and sci-fi she's left with a serious writing/drawing habit that just won't quit. These days, she spends much of her time writing, drawing, and chasing a very short Basset Hound named Sherlock.

When not, daydreaming up new characters to write and draw she can be found crocheting, making cute bookmarks, and binge-watching whatever happens to catch her eye.

Learn more about Lou and her future projects on her website: http://louinprogress.com/ or join her mailing list at: http://subscribepage.com/mailermailer

facebook.com/LouWilham

instagram.com/lou.wilham

MORE BOOKS YOU'LL LOVE

If you enjoyed this story,
please consider leaving a review.

Then check out more books from
Midnight Tide Publishing!

Apple of Fate by Elle Beaumont

Acontius desires the one thing in life he can't have—a soul mate. Raised by the Greek goddess, Artemis, Acontius swore an oath to serve her for eternity, and abstain from love.Centuries later, when Olympus has fallen, and the gods live amongst humankind, Acontius discovers a young woman who mirrors his loneliness and longing. Throwing caution to the wind, he tosses an apple at her feet, engraved with words that will bind them to one another.

Delia's life is in shambles. She's just lost her job, suffered through a recent breakup, and her health is declining. What she needs more than ever is a getaway trip to another country. But when she meets a playful museum worker,

Delia lets her walls down for once, which unwittingly sparks a goddess's ire.

With Delia's life hanging in the balance, Acontius must ensure she falls in love with him—or else she'll die, and he'll become another one of Artemis' hunting dogs for eternity.

Available on
5.19.21

Liars & Curses by Melissa Eskue Ousley

Hades hath no fury like a demigod scorned.

Penny has a penchant for curses. As well she should, since she's the immortal daughter of the legendary sorceress Circe and her lover Odysseus. (Yes, that Odysseus.) After walking the earth for centuries, Penny settles in New York, enjoying the Metropolitan Museum of Art and moonlit walks in Central Park. When she encounters a world-class liar who harms the man under her protection, not even the gods will be able to save the mortal from Penny's vengeance.

Available now

Ragnarok Unwound by Kristin Jacques

Prophecies don't untangle themselves.

Just ask Ikepela Ives, whose estranged mother left her with the power to unravel the binding threads of fate. Stuck with immortal power in a mortal body, Ives has turned her back on the duty she never wanted.

But it turns out she can't run from her fate forever, not now that Ragnarok has been set in motion and the god at the center of that tangled mess has gone missing. With a ragtag group of companions—including a brownie, a Valkyrie, and the goddess of death herself—Ives embarks on her first official mission as Fate Cipher—to save the world from doomsday.

Nothing she can't handle. Right?

Available now

www.ingramcontent.com/pod-product-compliance
Lightning Source LLC
Chambersburg PA
CBHW021741190726
48288CB00009B/3120